Nina Can...

RosAnne Tetz

Pacific Press Publishing Association
Boise, Idaho
Oshawa, Ontario, Canada

Edited by Aileen Andres Sox
Design and cover color by Tim Larson
Cover and interior art by James Converse
Typeset in 14/40 Times Roman

Unless otherwise noted, all Scripture quotations are taken from the International Children's Bible.

ISBN: 0-8163-1111-0

93 94 95 96 97 • 5 4 3 2 1

Nina

Baby Willy

Nina's Mama

Nina's Daddy

Jesus

Nina's Grandma

Nina's Grandpa

Andrew

Andrew's Mama

Cassie

Kitty

Aunt Brenda

Cousin Didi

Alberto's Mama

Alberto

NINA CAN PRAY

Never stop praying (1 Thessalonians 5:17).

 was all ready for . She had and .

She had her pajamas on. But was putting to , so could play a little longer.

 got her stuffed animals from their , her , her , and her . She got her from her . She sat them in a row and said, "Now we will at church." She "The Trees Are Gently Swaying" and "This Little Light of Mine."

 came in and said, "What pretty ! Are you ready for sleeping, 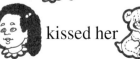?"

 kissed her 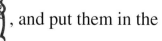, and put them in the .

"Good night, . Good night, . Good night, ."

held her and climbed into 's lap in the .

and read a . Then turned out the

, and they rocked while " Loves Me." "

loves you, ," said. "Let's talk to ."

"I can do it myself," said . "Dear , I love You too.

Amen."

5

NINA CAN PRACTICE

It is better to be patient (Ecclesiastes 7:8).

 came to visit. She brought a . brought a

 for too. said, "Thank you"; then she sat on the

floor and unwrapped her  . "It's a puzzle !" said.

 and went to look at 's nursery. stayed

on the floor and pushed the out of her new . There were a

lot of pieces . tried and tried, but she couldn't get any of the

back into the . So went and sat on 's lap while

 talked to .

When left, grabbed 's . "Please come

help me do my ."

6

"I need to start supper," said . Then she said, "Well, just one time."

 showed how to turn all the right side up so could see the colors, not the cardboard. Then showed how to look for the corners that have two flat sides. They put the four corner into the . Next they found the edge with one flat side and put them in. Then they put the last few in the middle.

"Now you practice, ," said , "while I make supper." practiced and practiced on her . 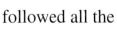 followed all the steps had taught her. And when came home, showed him how she could put her new together all by herself.

NINA CAN COOPERATE

Accept each other with love (Ephesians 4:2).

 and her family went to 's . After lunch

and drew with  on the driveway while everyone else sat on

the .

porch

"  ," called. " won't draw the . I

want him to draw the 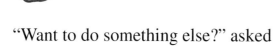 for my ."

"You're not the boss, ," said. "It's not fair for you to

tell what to do."

"Want to do something else?" asked .

"OK," said . got his 🚲 out of the garage.

and 🙂 drew a winding road on the driveway. Then 🙂 got on the

🚲, and 🙂 climbed on the back. He took her for a ride on their

8

road. Then they traded places, and took for a ride.

"Hang on tight, ," called. " is a wild driver."

It started to rain, so everyone came inside. "What shall we do now?"

 asked.

"It's your turn to choose," said. decided they should

set up his for and to watch.

In the on the way home said, "I had lots of fun."

"It's fun when you play together," said. "I'm glad you de-

cided to stop being bossy."

"And I'm sure is too!" laughed .

NINA CAN CHOOSE

You must choose for yourselves today (Joshua 24:15).

 gave  a . "It came from and ," she said. opened her 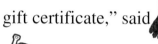. Inside was a piece of paper. "That's a gift certificate," said 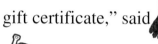. "You can take it to the store to get a . Maybe we can go after supper."

Before they went into the store, said, ", the store is only open for a little while longer. You will have to choose quickly."

 showed her some she could choose from. Finally picked out some . "You have a little bit of left," said . "Would you like to get some to blow to make laugh?"

"Good idea," said .

As they walked past the  store, said, "How about some

 ?"

"Good idea," said and .

 picked up so she could see. "What kind do you want,

honey?" he asked.

"Pink," said .

At time, told , "I like my and pink ."

"Yes, they were good choices," said . "Every day we make lots

of choices. Who's in that 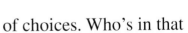 over your ?"

" ," answered .

"Every day we need to choose ," said .

 snuggled close to and whispered, "I choose ."

11

NINA CAN SURPRISE

The girl's parents were amazed (Luke 8:56).

 liked to play peekaboo. Over and over,  put his blanket over her head, then pulled it off and yelled, "Surprise!"  laughed and laughed every time.

After a while  realized it was quiet. She went to look.  was lying on the floor, chewing on his toes.  went to find .

 was in her room, painting. When she saw , she said, "Surprise!"  was surprised.  had  on her face and her hair and her . "I ed you a ,"  said.

"It's a beautiful ," said , "but next time you want to , let me help you put on your smock."  helped  change

her  and and s and clean the out of her hair.

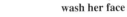
wash her face

"Would you like to make a surprise for ?" asked. "How

about a supper?"

 jumped up and down and sang, "Yes, yes, yes."

helped carry things out to the . When came

home, jumped into his arms and said, "Surprise, surprise! A

!"

As they all sat around the 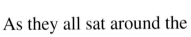, prayed, "Dear

, thank You for this and thank You for my wonderful,
food

surprising family. Amen."

NINA CAN FIX IT

The rest will I set in order when I come (1 Corinthians 11:34, KJV).

was looking for her toy . She pulled everything

out of her . came in. "What a big mess!" she said.

"Here it is!" held up her . But when

pushed the switch, the wouldn't go. " ,"

wailed, "my won't work!"

said, "You clean up the ; then I'll fix your ."

looked at her big mess. "It's too hard," she said.

"It will be hard work," agreed . "Call me when you're done."

sat down in the middle of the big mess. She flew her

around. Finally she flew the  right into the . That was fun.

She bounced her into the . Then she sailed her in.

She helped waddle in. Soon all the were back in the .

" ," called. "I'm ready."

came in with the . "Good job, sweetheart," she said. "I think your just needs a new battery." took

out the old battery and put a new battery in. "Try it now," said .

pushed the switch. The chugged away. "You fixed it!" cried.

"It's a good thing you fixed your room," said. "Or else your

would keep bumping into that big mess."

"We are good fixers," said 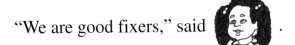 .

15

NINA CAN
DRESS HERSELF

You can be even more sure that God will clothe you (Matthew 6:30).

 dumped the of clothes on the big .

climbed up and began bouncing on the . They heard a buzzing noise

downstairs. "Oops, I better go get the out of the oven," said .

"Be careful. Don't bounce off the  ."

When came back up  and saw , she laughed.

 was playing dress-up with the clean clothes. She had on 's

 and 's , and she had a on her head. " ,

you look great," said . "You dressed yourself! What a big girl!"

16

The next morning, after _____ 's _____ , _____ said, "Would you like to dress yourself, honey? Come choose." _____ ran over to the dresser. "Which _____ do you like?" asked _____ .

"My teddy bear _____ ," said _____ _____ helped her pull it over her head; then _____ put her arms through the sleeves.

"Which _____ do you want?" asked _____ , "red or blue?"

"Red," said _____ , and she sat down and put her _____ in.

"Oops," said _____ . "You have 2 _____ , and the _____ have two holes. You need to put each leg in a different hole." She helped _____ pull up the back part of her _____ . Next _____ picked out her _____ and

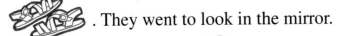 . They went to look in the mirror.

"I look great!" said _____ .

17

NINA CAN PRETEND

The Lord searcheth all hearts, and understandeth all the imaginations (1 Chronicles 28:9, KJV).

 went in to see if was awake. peeked over the and said, "Meow!"

"Oh, good morning, little ," said as she patted 's head. "How about some breakfast?"

"Yes, meow!" said 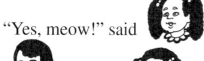.

 helped climb into her and pour a .

bowl of cereal

Then turned to help eat his breakfast. When looked back at , she was surprised. had her face in her . "I'm a ," said , with dripping down her chin.

18

"Well, why don't you pretend to be a very smart  that can eat with a ⎯⎯ ," said [girl] , and she wiped [baby] 's face.

After breakfast [girl] put [baby] in the [bathtub] . "I'm a [fish] ," said Nina, and she lay on her tummy and wiggled her [hand] s and [legs] .

"What a good swimmer!" said [girl] . "Little [baby] [fish] , could you help [baby boy] learn to sit in the [bathtub] ? I think he is big enough now." [girl] put [baby boy] in the [bathtub] . He laughed and splashed.

[baby] sat close to [baby boy] . "I'm an [angel] ," said [baby] . "I'll watch [baby boy] ."

[girl] laughed. "Thank you, [baby] [angel] ."

19

NINA CAN SAY HELLO

I hope to come visit you. Then we can be together and talk. That will make us very happy (2 John 12).

 and were playing after while and

 talked. Nina ran over to tell that she was hungry.

heard call and talk very fast. " , she talks fast,"

said . "I can't hear."

" is speaking Spanish, and you speak only English," said .
"Spanish is another language."

"Would you like to speak Spanish?" asked  . 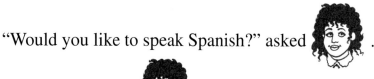 nodded.

"Say hola [*o-la*]," said . "That means hello."

"Hola," said .

"Hola. Very good," said .

"Hola, ," said .

"Hola, ," said .

 ran over and gave  a big hug. "Hola, ," she

shouted. Then she ran away while he chased her.

 scooped  up and carried her on his shoulders to the

. "Did you have fun at  today, ?"

asked.

"Yes," said 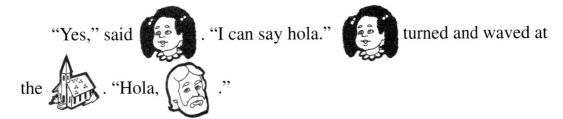. "I can say hola." 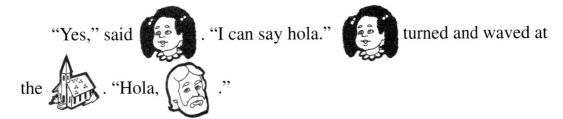 turned and waved at

the 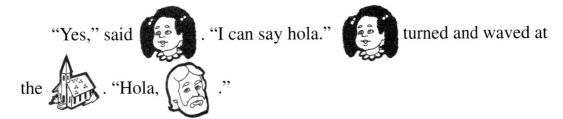. "Hola, 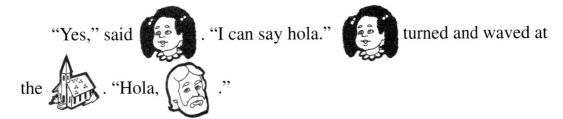."

21

NINA CAN SING

I will sing to the Lord all my life (Psalm 104:33).

"   ," said   , "please turn it over."

"Is your   finished?" asked   . "OK, I'll be right there."

   finished putting on   's   . While she snapped up

his   ,   sang a little made-up   about his tiny toes.

song

"What's that   ?" asked   .

"It's a tiny-toe   ," said   . "Now I'll sing it about your toes."

   watched   's   while she sang. "Sing it again, please,"

mouth

she said. So   sang again, this time about   's toes.

   fixed   's   so it would play again.   lis-

tened to the   while she played with her   and rolled on the rug.

When the stopped, ran to tell , but she was talking on the . While she waited, sang a about her missionary and flew it around the kitchen. " , I'm talking to your ," said. "She wants to know what that pretty is. Will you sing for her?"

put the phone by 's ear. sang the for . "That was just beautiful!" said . "Where did you learn that ?"

" ," said .

"You sound like an ," said . "I love to hear you sing."

"I love you," said . And she blew her a kiss.

23

NINA CAN SMELL

If the whole body were an ear, the body would not be able to smell anything (1 Corinthians 12:17).

When ▢ woke from her nap, ▢ said, "▢ is still

sleeping. Shall we make a surprise for ▢ ?"

"Yes," said ▢ . "Brownies!" ▢ helped unwrap the butter

and dump in the ▢ after ▢ measured it.

They were just putting the ▢ in the oven when ▢ said, "I

hear ▢ ." They went up ▢ . ▢ lifted ▢ up.

▢ sniffed. "Change ▢ 's ▢ ," ▢ said.

"Good idea," agreed ▢ . ▢ handed ▢ a clean ▢ .

They heard the door open. "▢ 's home!" yelled ▢ . She ran

24

down  and gave a big hug. "Why don't you and take

a quick walk around the block?" said to . " has a

surprise for you, and when you get back, it will be ready."

 hopped in her 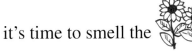 , and 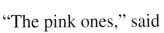 started pulling very fast.

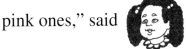 giggled, "Run, 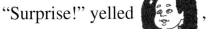 . Run."

When they were almost home,  said, "Whew, I'm tired. I think

it's time to smell the 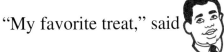 ." climbed out of her , and

they smelled the neighbor's . "Which color smells best?" asked .

"The pink ones," said .

When they came inside, said, "What's that wonderful smell?"

"Surprise!" yelled , "brownies!"

"My favorite treat," said . "And you are my favorite little ."

25

NINA CAN SIT STILL

He made the storm be still. He calmed the waves (Psalm 107:29).

When  came home from work,  was crying,  was rocking him in the , and  was climbing on 's back.

"Let's go out for supper," said .

 fell asleep in the , so  carried him into the restaurant in his ; then he stood in line to order the .

", choose which  you want to sit in," said . "Then you can tell me a story until  comes with our ."

 climbed onto a  and began jumping on it. "I'm a cowboy," she said.

"No, ," said . "Sit down."

"Why?" asked , still jumping.

"It's not safe," said , "and it might bother the other people who are trying to eat, and it might wake up ."

Then  fell off the  and began to cry.

 picked up  and held her close. "You'll be all right," she said. "You'd better get into your  again, only this time sit still."

 brought the  as  climbed into her .

"Would you like to talk to ?" asked .

"Thank You, , for this ," said . "And help me sit still." Then  sat in her  and ate all her  and drank all her .

NINA CAN TRAVEL

He has put his angels in charge of you. They will watch over you wherever you go (Psalm 91:11).

 got  out of  while it was still dark. "We're going on the  to see  today,"  whispered.  helped  put on her  and . Then they went outside to get in the .

 started to put  in her , but she said, "I can do it my-self."  let  climb into her ; then he buckled her in.

"Let's talk to ," said . He bowed his head. "Dear , please keep my family safe as they go on the  today. Amen."

 drove to the  station. He helped  carry the

28

, and he bought their tickets. Then he kissed , , and goodbye. "I'll see you in 2 days," said.

Soon it was time to get on the . "I have to hold and the ," told . "I want you to hold on tight to my ." was very careful to stay close to . They sat down in the first seat they could find. "Whew, isn't this exciting? Let's have a ," said as she got some out of her bag.

After breakfast they read some s; then they got up and walked around the . They found the little bathroom and got a drink of water at the fountain. Then said, "We get off at the next stop. We'd better get ready." As they got off the , saw and waiting for them. Everybody got hugs and kisses.

29

NINA CAN HUG

I wanted to gather them together as a hen gathers her chicks under her wings (Matthew 23:37).

 was lying on the , reading. crawled up and pulled on his . "Hi, ," she said.

"Hi, precious," said , and he gave her a hug. "Would you take this hug to for me?"

 climbed down and ran to find . She was talking on the . hugged her leg. "This hug is from ," she said.

 said, "Just a minute," into the . Then she said, "Thanks, . I'm talking to ."

"Give this hug," said, and she gave another hug.

talked into the . " 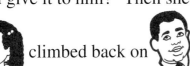 gave me a hug for .

Will you give it to him?" Then she winked at .

 climbed back on . "Any more hugs?" she asked.

"Of course." squeezed her tight. "Here is a big hug for you, and

a middle-sized hug for , and a tiny hug for ."

 was lying on the rug. gave him his middle-sized hug.

After she got her hug, ran under the . Then saw her

 of . She ran to . "I want to give a hug," said.

"What a wonderful idea," said. "You can't hug now, but

when He takes us to heaven, you can. Would you like to tell Him?"

 closed her eyes. "Dear ," she said. "I have a big hug for

You. Amen."

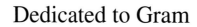

Dedicated to Gram